Doggie Data

Golden Retrievers

CHRISTA C. HOGAN

BLACK RABBIT BOOKS

Bolt is published by Black Rabbit Books
P.O. Box 227, Mankato, Minnesota, 56002.
www.blackrabbitbooks.com

Marysa Storm, editor; Catherine Cates, interior designer; Grant Gould, cover designer; Omay Ayres, photo researcher

Library of Congress Cataloging-in-Publication Data
Names: Hogan, Christa C., author.
Title: Golden retrievers / by Christa C. Hogan.
Description: Mankato, Minnesota : Black Rabbit Books, [2019] | Series: Bolt. Doggie data | Audience: Age 9-12. | Audience: Grade 4 to 6. | Includes bibliographical references and index.
Identifiers: LCCN 2017016589 (print) | LCCN 2017030562 (ebook) | ISBN 9781680725186 (ebook) | ISBN 9781680724028 (library binding) | ISBN 9781644662496 (paperback)
Subjects: LCSH: Golden retriever–Juvenile literature.
Classification: LCC SF429.G63 (ebook) | LCC SF429.G63 H64 2019 (print) | DDC 636.752/7-dc23
LC record available at https://lccn.loc.gov/2017016589

Image Credits

Alamy: Antonio Gravante, 7 (bttm); John Sirlin, 10–11; Steve Oehlenschlager, 13 (full pg); Dreamstime: Leloft1911, Cover (dog); iStock: bobbymn, 4–5; MarkCoffeyPhoto, 8–9; Science Source: John & Maria Kaprielian, 18; Shutterstock: 135pixels, 22; Africa Studio, 31; anetapics, 24 (bttm); Arthito, 20; Christian Mueller, 14; dogist, 23 (top); Eastimages, 21 (adult); Eric Isselee, 12–13 (bttm dogs), 16, 28; Frank11, 23 (bttm); HelgaMariah, 17 (rottie); Hollysdogs, 1; Javier Brosch, Cover (doghouse); Joop Snijder Photography, 10; KariDesign, 18–19; M88, 7 (full pg); Mat Hayward, 23 (top); Nataliya Sdobnikova, 17 (husky); Olena Brodetska, 21 (senior); Petr Jilek, 17 (full pg), 27; Rada Photos, 21 (adolescent); sergioboccardo, 32; tstockphoto, 3; USBFCO, 17 (retriever)
Every effort has been made to contact copyright holders for material reproduced in this book. Any omissions will be rectified in subsequent printings if notice is given to the publisher.

Contents

CHAPTER 1

Meet the Golden Retriever

A golden retriever and its owner walk through a park. Nearby, a family grills burgers. Down the path, a beagle barks. It wants to play. But the golden ignores the scents and sounds. It stays by its owner's side. The golden's owner is blind. And it is the dog's job to guide her.

Dog Jobs

Golden retrievers are gentle dogs. They make wonderful family pets. Goldens are also great helpers. They love to learn and work. Some goldens help police officers sniff out trouble. Others **assist disabled** people.

Goldens make excellent search and rescue dogs. They also work well as therapy and guide dogs.

PARTS OF A GOLDEN RETRIEVER

SILKY EARS
ATHLETIC BODY
STRONG LEGS

How Big Is a Golden Retriever?

HEIGHT
at shoulder
21.5 TO 24 INCHES
(55 to 61 centimeters)

CHAPTER 2

A Special Personality

Golden retrievers get along well with kids, other animals, and new people.

These cheerful dogs have a lot of energy. They may jump up on visitors or small kids. Owners must teach them to contain their energy.

Doggie Helpers

Goldens are also clever dogs. Their intelligence makes them easy to train. And many need jobs to be happy. Goldens' jobs can be simple. They can bring in newspapers for their owners. Goldens can also retrieve ducks for hunters. "Retriever" isn't part of their name for nothing.

TOP 10 MOST POPULAR Dogs in the United States in 2016

1 Labrador Retrievers

2 German Shepherds

3 Golden Retrievers

4 Bulldogs

5
Beagles
6
French Bulldogs
7
Poodles
8
Rottweilers
9
Yorkshire Terriers
10
Boxers

Goldens love to play fetch.

Happy Homes

Goldens can live in apartments or on farms. They don't need a lot of space to be happy. But they do need to be near people.

Goldens also need a lot of exercise. They love to run and play games. Many people say a tired golden is a happy golden. Bored or lonely goldens can get into mischief.

CHAPTER 3

Golden Retrievers' Features

Golden retrievers are medium-sized dogs. They weigh up to 75 pounds (34 kg).

Goldens' coats are cream or dark gold. Their tails are long and strong. Goldens have soft **muzzles** and friendly eyes.

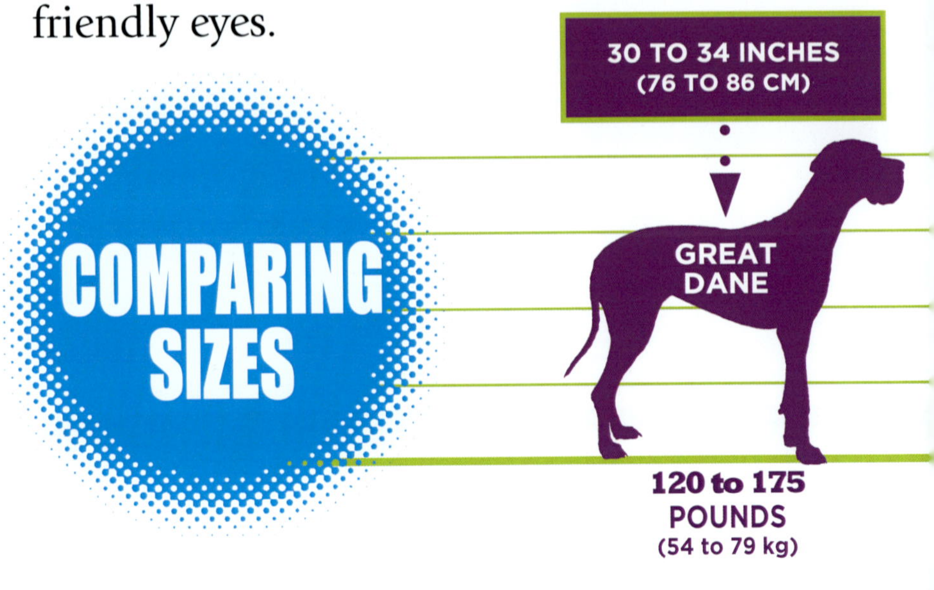

22 TO 27 INCHES
(56 TO 69 CM)
21.5 TO 24 INCHES
(55 to 61 CM)
20 TO 23.5 INCHES
(51 TO 60 CM)
ROTTWEILER
GOLDEN
RETRIEVER
SIBERIAN
HUSKY
85 to 135
POUNDS
(39 to 61 kg)
55 to 75
POUNDS
(25 to 34 kg)
35 to 60
POUNDS
(16 to 27 kg)

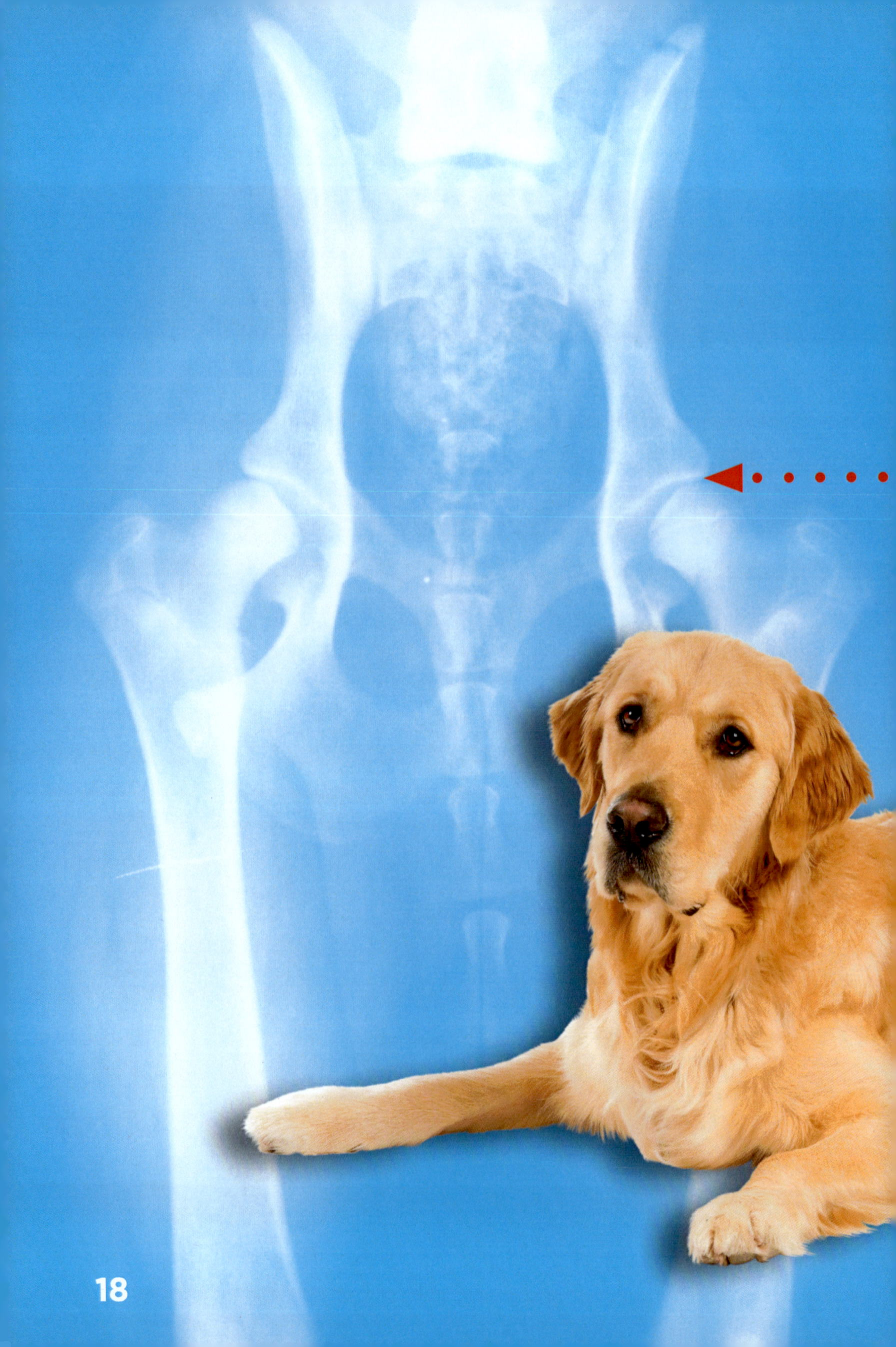

Golden Retriever Health

Most goldens are healthy. They can live for 12 to 14 years. But many large dogs have hip and elbow **dysplasia**. The condition can make walking painful. Goldens can also get **cataracts**. Cataracts make it hard for the dogs to see.

Goldens are more likely to get Von Willebrand's disease than other breeds. The disease is a bleeding disorder. It keeps blood from clotting.

Golden Retriever

Life Cycle

Newborn puppies weigh about 1 pound (.5 kg).

PUPPY

Senior goldens move more slowly and sleep more.

ADOLESCENT

Pups grow quickly from four to seven months old.

ADULT

Goldens reach their full height around one year. They still play like puppies, though.

SENIOR

CHAPTER 4

Caring for Golden Retrievers

Owning a golden takes work. Goldens have an outercoat and an undercoat. They shed all year long. Goldens need brushing at least once a week. This breed also has a strong doggy smell. They need a bath at least once a month.

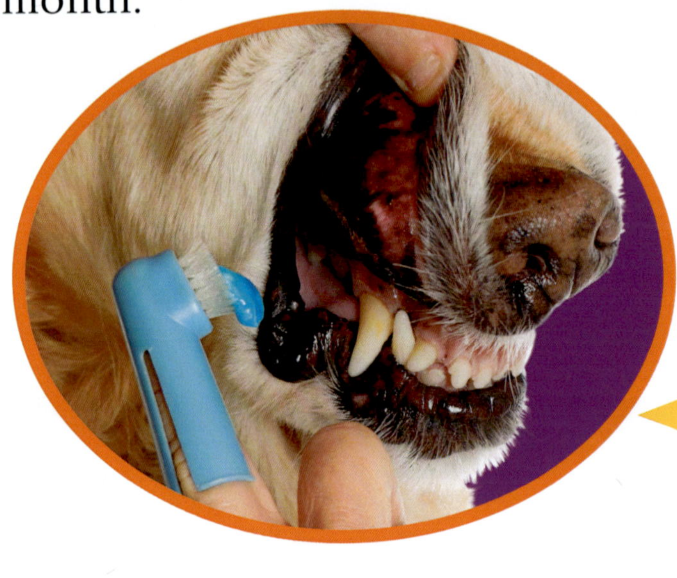

Grooming

bathing and brushing

nail trimming

teeth brushing

Good activities for goldens include going for runs, playing fetch, and swimming.

Eating and Exercising

Goldens love to eat. How much food they need depends on how much they exercise. If goldens overeat, they gain weight. Overweight goldens are more likely to have health problems.

Goldens are built to run and play. These dogs need about 30 minutes of exercise twice a day.

Cheerful and Smart Helpers

Goldens enjoy helping people and love their owners. Their friendly personalities make them lovable pets. They can need special medical care later in life. But owners say their pups are worth it.

Is a Golden Retriever Right for You?

Answer the questions below. Then add up your points to see if a golden is a good fit.

1 Do you mind hair and slobber on your things?

A. Yuck! Really? (1 point)
B. I like to keep things clean. (2 points)
C. Not at all. It means a dog lives here! (3 points)

2 Do you want a dog that follows you around?

A. No, I need my space. (1 point)

B. I like attention, but I'm fine on my own too. (2 points)

C. Aw, that sounds perfect! (3 points)

3 What's your favorite way to spend free time?

A. watching TV (1 point)

B. going shopping (2 points)

C. going to the park (3 points)

3 points

A golden is not your best match.

4–8 points

You like goldens, but another breed might be better for you.

9 points

A golden retriever would be a great buddy for your life!

GLOSSARY

adolescent (ad-oh-LES-uhnt)—a young person or animal that is developing into an adult

assist (uh-SIST)—to give support or help

cataract (KAT-uh-rakt)—a clouding of the lens of the eye or of the transparent cover around it that blocks the passage of light

clot (KLOT)—a mass or lump made by a liquid that thickens and sticks together

disabled (dys-A-buhld)—unable to perform one or more natural activities because of illness, injury, or other problems

disorder (dis-AWR-duhr)—an abnormal physical or mental condition

dysplasia (dys-PLA-zhuh)—an abnormal structure

muscular (MUS-kyu-lur)—having large and strong muscles

muzzle (MUH-zuhl)—the usually long nose and mouth of an animal

resistant (re-ZIS-tuhnt)—able to withstand the force or effect of something

therapy (THER-uh-pee)—the treatment of physical or mental illnesses

BOOKS

Bowman, Chris. *Golden Retrievers.* Awesome Dogs. Minneapolis: Bellwether Media, 2016.

Bozzo, Linda. *I Like Golden Retrievers!* Discover Dogs with the American Canine Association. New York: Enslow Publishing, 2017.

Finne, Stephanie. *Golden Retrievers.* Dogs. Minneapolis: Checkerboard Library, an imprint of Abdo Publishing, 2015.

WEBSITES

Dog Breed Selector
www.animalplanet.com/breed-selector/dog-breeds.html

Golden Retriever Dog
www.ducksters.com/animals/golden_retriever.php

Golden Retriever Dog Breed Information
www.akc.org/dog-breeds/golden-retriever/

INDEX